Novato Teen New
Teen Fiction
McClintoc
Back
31111029083407

W9-BDX-098

Back

Back

Norah McClintock

orca soundings

ORCA BOOK PUBLISHERS

Copyright © 2009 Norah McClintock

All rights reserved. No part of this publication may be reproduced
or transmitted in any form or by any means, electronic or mechanical, including
photocopying, recording or by any information storage
and retrieval system now known or to be invented, without
permission in writing from the publisher.

Library and Archives Canada Cataloguing in Publication

McClintock, Norah
Back / Norah McClintock.

(Orca soundings)
ISBN 978-1-55143-991-4 (bound).--ISBN 978-1-55143-989-1(pbk.)

I. Title. II. Series: Orca soundings

PS8575.C62B33 2009   jC813'.54   C2008-908027-0

Summary: After serving time for a violent crime, Jojo returns to the
neighborhood and tries to take his life back.

First published in the United States, 2009
Library of Congress Control Number: 2008943122

Orca Book Publishers gratefully acknowledges the support for its publishing
programs provided by the following agencies: the Government of Canada
through the Book Publishing Industry Development Program and the Canada
Council for the Arts, and the Province of British Columbia through the BC Arts
Council and the Book Publishing Tax Credit.

Cover design by Teresa Bubela
Cover photography by Getty Images

ORCA BOOK PUBLISHERS
PO Box 5626, STN. B
VICTORIA, BC CANADA
V8R 6S4

ORCA BOOK PUBLISHERS
PO Box 468
CUSTER, WA USA
98240-0468

www.orcabook.com
Printed and bound in Canada.
Printed on 100% PCW recycled paper.
12 11 10 09 • 4 3 2 1

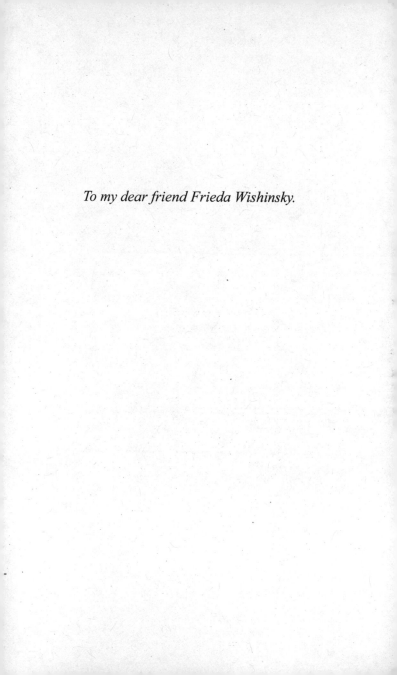

To my dear friend Frieda Wishinsky.

Chapter One

It's summer and I'm sidelined with a broken ankle. I'm thinking I'm in for the most boring summer of my life until the word gets around that Jojo Benn is coming back home to live with his mother. Everyone knows he's coming back a few days before he actually shows up because his mother tells Megan Dalia's mom. Megan's mom immediately tells everyone else, even though she says she doesn't blame Jojo's mother for what he did. My mother has a different opinion. She says

Jojo's mother was always too soft on him. She says Jojo would have turned out differently if he had been taken in hand.

Jojo is twenty when he comes back. While we wait, we all wonder if he will show up in a taxi or if maybe one of his old friends, who haven't been around much while Jojo has been away, will drive him up to his mother's front door.

But he doesn't arrive in a taxi or a car. Instead, a city bus slides to a stop at the end of the street, and Jojo gets off. He's carrying a suitcase. He's taller than anyone remembers. He's bulkier too. Some people say it's from all the bad food he probably ate while he was locked up. Other people say they heard that guys work out in there, and sure enough, when Jojo walks past my house carrying his suitcase, I see muscles on his arms that I never saw before.

Jojo doesn't look at anyone, but everyone sure looks at him. He walks up to the front door of his mother's house and rings the bell. Someone opens the door, and he goes inside. After that—only after that—people come off their porches and into the street and start talking.

There are a lot of people who can't believe that Jojo has had the nerve to come back to our neighborhood. There are more people who don't want him around. Things haven't exactly been peaceful since he went away. Things are never peaceful in my neighborhood. But at least people haven't worried about Jojo for the past two years.

I know Jojo, but I don't know him well. He lives in the same row of houses that I live in. His mother is our next-door neighbor. Jojo is nearly four years older than me, so we never hung out together. But I used to see him out in his backyard sometimes when the weather was nice, making some food on the barbecue or sitting in the sun or fooling around with some of his friends. Sometimes he would be talking to his mother who, it would surprise a lot of people to know, he always talked nice to. Because I saw him like that and other people didn't, I could see that sometimes he seemed like just a regular person. But then he'd get out on the street with his friends, and he'd do bad things—hurt people or humiliate them or take their stuff. Everyone was glad when he went away. Everyone except his mother.

Now he's back, and people are tense and afraid. They wonder if his friends will start showing up again. They wonder if they'll be walking down the street one day and they'll run into Jojo and he will give them attitude or shove them around, just for fun. They wonder if he'll show up in their stores or their restaurants and take stuff and tell them, *Go ahead, call the cops*, which a lot of them are afraid to do (Jojo always seems to know which ones are afraid) because Jojo's friends have a way of making it hard—really hard—on people who decide to press charges against Jojo. Those people just wish Jojo would go away and never come back.

Then there are the people who have hate in their hearts. Those people wish something bad would happen to Jojo. Something really bad.

Ardell Withrow is one of those people.

Chapter Two

Ardell Withrow's brother Eden is the reason Jojo got sent away. Eden is one year older than Ardell. He is—*was*—an okay guy. He graduated high school and was about to do something that no one else in his family had ever done. He was about to go to college. Then he pissed off Jojo. I didn't see it, but I heard what happened.

Jojo used to go with a girl named Shana, right up until he got Shana pregnant. He wanted Shana to get rid of the baby. Shana refused. She told Jojo she was going to have it and raise it and if he didn't like it, that was his problem. Jojo didn't like that. He didn't like anyone making a decision about *his* kid, never mind that he didn't want the kid in the first place. He didn't like Shana, or anyone else for that matter, telling him no when he wanted to hear yes. He particularly didn't like Shana telling him that what she did with her body was none of his business.

So Jojo did what he always did when he didn't care for someone's attitude—he made life hard for Shana. He called her names—slut and whore and worse—whenever he saw her. He talked about her to his friends. He told them personal stuff about what he and Shana used to do when they were together. He muscled her and, one time, grabbed her breast right out there in the street. When Shana slapped his face for that, he slapped her back five times harder.

Then, one day, while Shana was on the way down the street past his house to get to her own house half a block away, Jojo and his friends surrounded her. There must have been six or seven of them. They boxed her in, and Jojo started calling her names and saying how miserable the baby's life was going to be with her for its mother. The whole time, Shana didn't say a word. That only made Jojo angrier. Finally he shoved her off the curb. Shana had a big belly by then. The baby was only one month away from being born.

Shana would have fallen and hurt herself, and maybe the baby, if it hadn't been for Eden Withrow. Eden was watching Jojo from across the street. When he saw Jojo and his friends circle Shana, he started to cross the street. He got there just in time to grab Shana's arm so that she didn't get knocked to the ground.

Jojo didn't like that either. He jumped Eden in an alley that night and beat him good with a crowbar. Eden was rushed by ambulance to the hospital emergency room. Then he was rushed into an operating room. From there he went to intensive care. He's still in the hospital—a different one now, one where they look after people who are never going to be able to make it on their own.

My mother, who knows Ardell's mother, says that people used to talk to Ardell's mother about Eden all the time. Then, when they found out that he would probably never wake up from the coma he was in, everyone stopped talking about him. But they're talking about him again now, and they all say the same thing. They all say that it's not right that Jojo only got five years, out in two, for taking away from Eden everything that makes a life worth living.

Ardell has been saying the same thing a lot, ever since we got word that Jojo was coming back. Another thing Ardell has been saying a lot: he's not afraid of Jojo. And I bet he isn't. First of all, Ardell has hate in his heart, and hate takes the fear out of people and replaces it with a thirst for vengeance. Second, Ardell hasn't been wasting his time. While everyone else has been breathing easier and probably hoping never to set eyes on Jojo again, Ardell has been applying himself to the study of martial arts. He's been bulking up too. His muscles are bigger than Jojo's.

It's almost as if Ardell has been wishing the opposite of everyone else. Everyone else wants peace and quiet, which means no Jojo. Ardell, though, he's hungry. He wants Jojo. He wants him bad, and now that he's back, Ardell is watching him. Everyone else is steering clear. They're wondering who Jojo will go after. They keep their eyes down, the way people do when they come across a big dog they don't know. They won't look that dog in the eye because they know the dog will see that as a challenge, and then, before they can even think of backing away, they'll be in a fight they can't win.

For a couple of days, everyone holds their breath. For the same couple of days, Jojo doesn't make a move. Then, I guess, Ardell decides he can't wait any longer.

Chapter Three

Ardell is following in his brother's footsteps. In the fall, he will become the first person in his family to go to college. He was supposed to be away this summer, working at the same camp for kids that he worked at last summer. But the camp burned down, and now Ardell doesn't have a job. He's been looking for one, but it's tough this year. Most of the summer jobs have already been taken. So mostly Ardell sits around on his porch and hangs out with his friends who don't have jobs or who are between shifts.

Ardell is a good guy, like his brother. Everyone says so. But the look in Ardell's eyes the first couple of days that Jojo is home is not the look you usually see in a good guy's eyes.

For the first couple of days, Jojo stays mostly in his mother's house. The people on my street tense up the second day when some of Jojo's old friends show up. But they stay in the house with Jojo. They don't go out onto the street. And after they leave, they don't come back again. Nobody knows why.

Finally, three days after Jojo gets back, his front door opens. It's the middle of July. It's hot. A lot of people are out on their porches. Other people are down on the sidewalk, talking, while they water their postage-stamp-sized front yards and the plants and flowers in their flowerbeds or in baskets hanging from their porch railings.

Ardell is out on his porch. He's just sitting there on a chair, watching Jojo's mother's house. When Jojo comes outside, Ardell stands up. When Jojo goes down his front walk to the sidewalk, Ardell crosses to his porch steps. When Jojo walks past Ardell's house, heading for the stores on the corner, Ardell comes down his walk. People all up and down the street turn to watch as Ardell swings onto the sidewalk and falls into step behind Jojo. You can practically hear people suck in their breath, like they're afraid of what's going to happen next.

But nothing happens.

Jojo is wearing sneakers that make no noise when he walks. Ardell is wearing boots, even in the summer heat. He sounds like the entire Russian army marching in step behind Jojo. But Jojo doesn't even turn around. He walks straight to the ice-cream store and goes inside.

Ardell waits outside. He's standing a couple of feet from the door, still waiting, when Jojo comes out carrying a plastic bag. Ardell looks right at Jojo, but Jojo doesn't look at Ardell. He walks past him and goes back up the street to his mother's house.

Ardell and his Russian army boots clomp back up the street behind Jojo and stop on the sidewalk outside Jojo's mother's house.

Jojo goes directly inside. Ardell stands on the sidewalk. People watch from their porches and their steps and their lawns until it becomes clear that nothing is going to happen. Then they go back about their business.

I go inside. Through the kitchen window, I see Jojo come out the sliding doors and onto the deck at the back of his mother's house. His mother is out there on a recliner. She looks smaller than she used to before Jojo went away.

Jojo puts the plastic bag from the ice-cream store onto a table that has an umbrella over it. He sets down a bowl and a spoon. He takes a container of ice cream out of the bag. He opens it and scoops some ice cream into the bowl, which he hands to his mother. She smiles at him when he gives her the bowl and the spoon. Her hand moves slowly from the bowl to her mouth. She seems to be putting a lot of effort into it, as if she is handling a shovel full of gravel instead of a spoonful of vanilla ice cream. But she gets it there. She swallows it, and she smiles again.

The whole time, Jojo has an eager, little-kid look on his face, like it really matters to him whether his mother likes the ice cream or not. It's not a mean or menacing smile. It's not a smile that says *I'm better than you* or *I'm going to get a lot of pleasure out of hurting you*. It's not a smile that says *You'd better watch out because one of these days…* It's not a smile you'd ever expect to see on Jojo's face. It's a smile that says *I made you happy, and I'm glad*.

His mother beckons to him, and he goes to her. She crooks her finger, and he bends down. She kisses him on the cheek, and Jojo smiles. I wonder what Ardell would say about that.

Chapter Four

Ardell is out on his porch again the next morning. I see him sitting there with a mug of coffee and the newspaper. But the newspaper is folded on his lap. He doesn't read it. He doesn't go through the employment ads. He's probably afraid that if he looks at the newspaper, he will miss Jojo.

People are watching. Quite a few people on my street work. Some, like my mother, work during the day. My mother is up at five thirty in the morning on workdays, getting my lunch ready before she leaves for the hospital, where she is a cleaner. She starts at seven in the morning and finishes at three thirty. If they ask her to stay on for an extra shift or even a few extra hours, she always says yes. "It's not like we don't need the money," she says.

Other people on the street work in the evening. Some work at night. And a lot of people don't work at all—they're too old or they're sick or they got hurt and can't work anymore. Some can't find a job. Some have given up looking. Some, like me, are waiting for summer to end. I'd rather be working, but just try to find a job when you've got a cast on your foot, even a walking cast like mine, and you have to tell your boss that you can't stand all day. At least school will give me something to do.

No matter what time of day it is, there are always people sitting on their porches, or standing on the sidewalk talking to other people, or across the street on their neighbors' porches, drinking coffee and talking. Because it's one of those nice July mornings—not too hot, and there's a breeze—a lot of people are outside. So a lot of people see Shana come up the street pushing a stroller.

Shana doesn't live on our street anymore, but her parents do. They live on the opposite side of the street from Jojo's mother, but half a block up. Shana comes every week to see them. She gets off the bus up at the corner where the stores are. She's so pretty that usually another passenger—nine times out of ten it's a man—helps her get the stroller off the bus. Then she walks up the street, pushing the stroller and showing off her son to everyone who happens to be outside. Most of the time she stops by Jojo's mother's house to visit Jojo's mother. Shana's parents don't like this. They don't like it at all. But Shana tells them that her son has the right to see all of his grandparents, not just some of them.

Everyone who is outside that day, including Ardell and me, watches Shana push that stroller up the street. Everyone is wondering if she will stop at Jojo's mother's house. Everyone is wondering if she even knows that Jojo is back. Maybe her parents haven't told her. Maybe they don't want her to know. Maybe they want to protect her and the baby.

Shana pushes the stroller to the end of the walk that leads to Jojo's mother's house. She looks up at the bright blue front door, the gleaming windows and the crisp white curtains. My mother says Jojo's mother is house-proud. Shana looks from the house to her son. She wheels the stroller onto the front walk and pushes it right up to the porch steps. She leaves it there at the bottom of the steps and goes up alone to ring the doorbell.

Jojo answers.

I'm on my porch, which is right next to Jojo's porch. There's just a small railing that separates them. I'm sitting there, catching the breeze and reading a magazine I borrowed from the library. I keep my head down, as if I'm still reading, but I can hear everything that's happening. I watch too, without being obvious about it.

I see Ardell, across the street, stand up and come to his porch railing so that he can get a better view of Jojo's mother's house.

I see Jojo look at Shana, his eyes wide, like he can't believe she is standing there at his door. I see him look around her and down the steps to the stroller. I see something I never thought I'd ever see. I see Shana smile at Jojo and say, "Do you want to meet your son?"

Jojo stares at her. More than anything, he looks surprised—maybe by the fact that Shana is even there after he pushed her that time, or maybe by the fact of his little son. He says, "I heard you named him Benjamin." Benjamin is the name of one of Shana's grandfathers.

Shana reaches for Jojo's hand. She catches it and leads him down the steps. She bends over to undo the buckle on the harness that's holding her son in the stroller. Then things get complicated.

The first thing that happens is that Ardell comes off his porch and crosses the street.

"My brother is in the hospital in a coma from defending you from that piece of garbage," he says to Shana. "If my brother hadn't helped you, that piece of garbage would have hurt you, and that baby might not even have been born. That piece of garbage isn't fit to be anyone's father."

Jojo just looks at him.

"But he *is* someone's father," Shana says.

Then Shana's father appears. I'm not sure how or even where he comes from because I've been looking over at Jojo's mother's house. But there he is, grabbing the stroller with the baby still in it and trying to turn it around. Shana puts her hands on the stroller's handles to stop him, but he pushes her away.

Jojo steps forward just like that, like it's an automatic thing, like he isn't even thinking about it. Shana's father, who has gray hair and deep wrinkles on his forehead, looks evenly at Jojo and says, "You going to put me in a coma too?"

Jojo throws his hands up in a gesture of surrender. He steps back a pace. I look up and down the street and see surprise on every face.

Every face except Ardell's. Ardell's eyes are filled with hate.

Shana bends down again, and this time she undoes the harness that's holding

Benjamin in. She picks him up and holds him out to Jojo. Jojo looks at Shana's father. He looks at Ardell. Then he looks at Benjamin. The boy smiles at Jojo. Jojo stretches out his arms, and the next thing you know, the most notorious person on my street seems amazed to find himself holding a chubby little boy. His very own son. He smiles at the child. His son smiles back. Then, looking embarrassed, Jojo hands him back to Shana. She buckles the boy back into the stroller.

"How's your mother?" she says when she straightens up again.

Jojo just shrugs.

Shana looks at her father, all sharp-faced and angry. She says to Jojo, "Tell her I'll come by next week."

Jojo nods.

Shana takes control of the stroller. She pushes it past Ardell, who says, "My brother is in a coma, and for what? For what?"

Shana's father puts a protective arm around Shana. He looks like he's as angry with Ardell as he is with Jojo. I hear him tell Shana, "You should stay away from here for a while."

Shana doesn't answer. She pushes the stroller down the sidewalk toward the house where she grew up. Jojo watches her. Then he goes back inside, leaving Ardell alone on the sidewalk.

Ardell glowers up at Jojo's mother's house. He wants to get even with Jojo. I can see it. Everyone can see it.

Chapter Five

Ardell goes three times a week most weeks to see his brother in the hospital. Ardell's mother goes four times a week most weeks, on the days Ardell doesn't go. Sometimes the two of them go together.

Ardell's father, who moved out of the house over a year ago, never goes. He told Ardell's mother, "What's the point? You heard what they said. He's never going to change." He told her, "We should let him go." That's when Ardell's mother decided to let Ardell's father go instead.

A week after Jojo gets out and comes back to live in his mother's house, the word on the street is this: Ardell's father has talked to Eden's doctor. Everybody already knows that Eden has irreversible brain damage. Everyone already knows that Eden probably won't come out of his coma. Now Ardell's father has talked to the doctor about turning off all the machines and letting Eden go.

This makes Ardell furious. He curses his father up and down the street.

"Let him go?" he says. "He means kill him. He means pull the plug. He calls himself a father. He says he just has Eden's best interests at heart. But he never goes to see him. Eden is already dead to him, and now he wants to make it official. He wants to kill him."

People talk about it all up and down the street.

People say, "If it's true what the doctors say, if he's never going to wake up, isn't it better to just let him go?"

Other people say, "He's alive. He's been alive for two years. You never know what medical science will be able to do a year or two or even five years from now. What if they pull the plug and then six months from now they come up with something that could have helped him? What then?"

Still other people say, "Jojo Benn should have been locked up for the rest of his life for what he did. He as good as killed that boy. An eye for an eye, that's what the Bible says. An eye for an eye."

Ardell never comes out and says it, but everyone knows that he's an eye-for-an-eye kind of person, at least where Jojo is concerned. He wants his brother to live. He wants his brother to wake up. But more than anything, he wants Jojo to pay for what he did. Instead Jojo is living right across the street in his mother's house. Every morning, Ardell is there to see Jojo come out, pick up the newspaper off the porch and carry it back inside to his mother. Every day, Ardell sees Jojo walk down to the store to buy food for his mother.

And then something happens.

Ardell's father arrives in his dusty old car. He parks it at the curb and starts up the walk to the porch. Ardell is out on the porch watching Jojo's mother's house. He blocks his father's way. Everyone on the street can hear him clearly as he says to his father, "Where do you think you're going?"

Ardell's father talks more quietly than Ardell. I only know what he said because one of Ardell's next-door neighbors told me. Ardell's father says, "I'm here to see your mother."

"She doesn't want to talk to you," Ardell says.

"It's important," his father says. "It's about your brother."

"He's still alive, if that's what you want to know," Ardell says.

Ardell's father shakes his head. He tries to get around Ardell, but Ardell is like a star basketball player. He keeps blocking his father.

Then the door to Jojo's mother's house opens, and Jojo steps out onto the porch.

He's carrying a big cotton shopping bag that his mother always takes with her when she goes shopping. Jojo's mother doesn't like to bring things home in plastic shopping bags. She says she doesn't believe in that.

At the same time, my mother comes to the door and says to me, "We're out of milk. Be an angel—go to the store and get me some." She hands me some money and goes back inside. She doesn't even notice what's going on on the other side of the street.

Ardell's father has seen Jojo. He has turned around one hundred and eighty degrees, as if he's completely forgotten that he has been trying to get into the house to see his wife. Instead, he's staring at Jojo. His jaw hangs open. Without taking his eyes off Jojo, he says to Ardell, "What's *he* doing here? What's that murderer doing back here?"

Ardell turns on his father the same hate-filled eyes he uses on Jojo. Ardell's neighbor, who saw the whole thing up close, said that you could tell Ardell was conflicted. On the one hand, he hated his father for calling Jojo a murderer because the person his father meant as the murder victim was Eden, and Eden wasn't dead. Ardell was fighting alongside his mother to keep Eden alive. But, on the other hand, somewhere deep inside, it looked like maybe Ardell knew his father was right, that Eden might never wake up, because he put a hand on his father's shoulder, and instead of arguing with him, he said, "He's here, but he's not staying." The neighbor who heard this isn't shy about repeating it all up and down the street.

Meanwhile, Jojo comes down his front walk with his mother's shopping bag. I decide to follow him. After all, my mom wants me to go to the store for milk.

I clomp down the sidewalk behind Jojo, moving slowly because of my walking cast. Jojo keeps his eyes straight ahead. If he knows I'm behind him, he doesn't let on. He goes to the small grocery store on the corner. It happens to be the same store I'm going to. It's not one of those chain grocery stores, but it sells everything we ever need, and my mother says the prices are fair.

Jojo goes into the store. Mr. Brisebois,

who owns the store and who you always see first thing up there at the cash, turns to look at him. As soon as he sees Jojo, he beckons to one of his daughters, who all work at the store. She comes and replaces him at the cash. Mr. Brisebois makes his way out from behind the counter and trails Jojo up and down the aisles. He does it right out in the open. He doesn't even try to pretend that he isn't following Jojo. I guess I can't blame him.

Mr. Brisebois is like a lot of the store owners in my neighborhood. He knows a lot of stores can't be bothered to set up here because people don't have a lot of money. He also knows that a lot of people don't have cars and that it's a pain to take the bus to go grocery shopping. So he knows he can make a good living here. But he's also wary. He knows that there are a lot of good, honest people in the neighborhood. But there are also people who aren't so good or honest. Some of them, like Jojo back before he sent Eden Withrow to the hospital, have given Mr. Brisebois a hard time. So Mr. Brisebois isn't shy. When people like Jojo come into his store, he follows them to make sure that they don't steal anything. Or he makes them so uncomfortable that they go somewhere else where maybe they can get away with stealing.

Jojo reaches for some cans of tomatoes. That's when he sees Mr. Brisebois standing behind him. Jojo straightens up. He turns and looks at Mr. Brisebois. Jojo is taller and bulkier than Mr. Brisebois. He's younger and in better shape. People are actually afraid of Jojo. No one is afraid of Mr. Brisebois, other than being afraid he might call the cops.

Mr. Brisebois stands his ground. He looks Jojo in the eye. He's not giving an inch, but he has one hand behind his back, and I can see that it's shaking.

Jojo looks at Mr. Brisebois. Then he walks a little farther down the aisle and pulls a package of dried spaghetti off the shelf. Mr. Brisebois is right with him. He follows Jojo to the cheese aisle, where Jojo picks up a can of shake-on Parmesan cheese. Then to the bread aisle, where Jojo picks up a loaf of crusty bread. Then to the produce aisle, where he picks up tomatoes, lettuce, a green pepper, some green onions and some garlic. Jojo carries it all to the cash, where Mr. Brisebois's daughter rings it through. The whole time, Mr. Brisebois watches her, and Jojo acts like Mr. Brisebois isn't there. He packs all the groceries in his mother's cloth shopping bag. He pays. He leaves the store.

Mr. Brisebois puts a hand on the counter and watches Jojo go through the door. He uses that hand to steady himself. He is perspiring a lot. He says to his daughter, "That one is no good. I wish he would shop somewhere else."

Mr. Brisebois's daughter says, "Why don't you tell him that?"

Mr. Brisebois goes back behind the cash to ring up my container of milk. His hands are shaking as he makes change from the bill my mother gave me.

"That one is no good," he says again. "Now that he's back, they'll all be back. Things will change."

Chapter Six

Things do change. But they don't change the way Mr. Brisebois thinks.

Back before Jojo was sent away, he used to hang out with guys who were just like him. They were big and smart-assed and into stuff they shouldn't have been. They had swagger and muscle and liked to use them both. They acted like they were in charge, like they were better than everyone else. They took what they wanted, and they dared you to do something about it.

Some people did do something. They called the cops for stuff like shoplifting. Something bad usually happened to people who ratted on Jojo. Their windows got broken or a fire broke out in their back alleys or someone dragged a nail up and down the sides of their cars. No one ever saw those things happen. The cops asked questions, but they never made an arrest because they were never able to prove anything. So after a while, if Jojo or one of his friends wanted a pack of smokes, they got it, free. If they wanted an ice cream from the ice-cream truck, they got it, until the guy who owned the ice-cream truck stopped coming around the neighborhood. The people who gave them free stuff called it insurance—you pay to insure that nothing bad is going to happen. Nothing bad that you can't prove and that the cops can't do anything about, but that leaves you out of produce or with expensive repairs to do and that scares you or your wife or kids.

Before I know it, Jojo has been back for a week, and apart from that one day, his friends don't come around. Jojo mostly stays at home. The weather stays nice, so he takes meals out to his mother, who sits out back under the big umbrella, sleeping. I hear kitchen sounds—pots and dishes—through the open window. I smell cooking smells. And still Jojo's mother is outside under that umbrella, which means that Jojo is doing the cooking. I hear the vacuum run in Jojo's house and see his mother outside under that umbrella, which means that Jojo is doing the cleaning. I have to think that over—Jojo doing all the housework. It makes me wonder what it must have been like where he has been. It makes me wonder what might have happened to him in there.

A few more days go by, and still Jojo's friends don't show up.

But Ardell's friends do.

Ardell has a lot of friends, and they have all grown in the time since Jojo was sent away. They are big and strong, but people don't see them as troublemakers. Mr. Brisebois doesn't follow any of them around his store. People never watch them and wonder what they are going to do. At least not until one morning two weeks after Jojo has been back.

That day Jojo comes out of the house. Ardell is across the street on his porch, as usual, except that the porch is crowded with Ardell's friends. They all come down off the porch behind Ardell. I count them—there are nine of them in addition to Ardell. They fall into line behind Jojo.

That gets people's attention up and down the street. It gets my attention too. I start to follow them. A lot of other people do too. Some of them follow directly behind Ardell and his friends. Others follow on the other side of the street, like me. But we all end up in the same place. We all end up on the sidewalk outside Mr. Brisebois's grocery store.

This time Ardell doesn't stay behind Jojo. Instead, he hurries around him and blocks his way into the store. His friends stand in a circle around Jojo.

All of Ardell's friends are tensed up. So is Ardell. Everyone is watching, even Mr. Brisebois, through the window of his store. Jojo just stands there. For a couple of moments he looks at Ardell. Then, very slowly, he turns around, the full three hundred and sixty degrees, looking at all nine of Ardell's friends one by one, until finally he is looking at Ardell again. For the first time since he has come back, Jojo says something in public.

"I don't want trouble," he says. "I just came to get some groceries."

Ardell doesn't move. He looks hard at Jojo. "You're not welcome here," he says.

Jojo looks over his right shoulder, and the guys who are standing on that side of him tense up, like they are afraid Jojo is going to lash out at them. Jojo looks over his left shoulder, and the guys who are standing on that side tense up. Then he looks at Ardell.

"If you want groceries," Ardell says, "you're going to have to go somewhere else to get them."

Behind Ardell, Mr. Brisebois moves from the window to the door of his store. He turns the lock and flips over the *OPEN* sign so that now it says *CLOSED, please call again*. Ardell smiles when he sees that. Mr. Brisebois moves back, away from the door.

"Looks like there are no groceries in there for you," Ardell says.

He pushes Jojo. The palms of both hands slam into Jojo's chest. Jojo stumbles backward. Someone sticks out a foot. Jojo trips on it and lands on his butt on the pavement. All the guys with Ardell laugh. Then Ardell kicks Jojo, hard. Someone else moves in and swings back a leg, but Jojo scrambles to his feet and darts between two of Ardell's friends so that now he's on the outside of the circle instead of on the inside. Ardell and his friends turn to go after him.

Then a double miracle happens. The first part of the miracle: a cop car slides around the corner with two cops in it, both of them with their eyes hidden behind sunglasses, but you know they are taking note of everything. The cops who ride through my neighborhood are always on the lookout for things that don't look right. A bunch of big muscle guys moving down the street after just one guy doesn't look right.

The second part of the miracle: the cop car doesn't mean trouble for Jojo. This time, maybe for the first time, the cops actually save Jojo. Ardell hangs back. Ardell's friends hang back. Jojo stumbles down the street to his mother's house. After the cop car disappears, people start to jeer, but by then Jojo is safe inside.

Chapter Seven

After the day when Ardell and his friends made a circle around Jojo, it seems that no one has anything better to do than be out there on the street to see what will happen next. Will Jojo call up his old friends? Will they come over and back him up the way they used to before he went away? Will it come down to Ardell on one side of the street and Jojo on the other, each with his own gang of friends? Will it come down to a real battle—and if it does, who will win? And then what will happen?

The next day Jojo doesn't come out of the house at all. I go out back at my house and look over the fence. Jojo's mother doesn't come out either, even though it's one of those nice days, warm but not too hot, not sticky either, with a nice breeze to cool you down.

The day after that, late in the afternoon, after everyone has seen Ardell and his mother walk down to the bus together, Jojo shows his face. He walks down the street to where the stores are. People drift down the street after him, as if they are curious about something. But what? Ardell isn't there. Nothing can happen. But people follow, which makes me curious. So I follow the people who are following Jojo.

Jojo walks directly to Mr. Brisebois's grocery store. Just as he gets to the door, Mr. Brisebois turns the lock and flips the sign in the door to *CLOSED*. Jojo looks through the glass at him. Then he looks down the block to the convenience store. He starts to walk toward it. Before he gets there, a *CLOSED* sign appears in the window. Three blocks down, there's a small fruit and vegetable store. It's always open, even on holidays when Mr. Brisebois's store is closed. But by the time Jojo gets to it, it's closed. Jojo hammers on the door. No one answers.

Jojo turns and looks at all the people who are watching him. A kid picks up a rock and throws it at him. He misses, but that's not the main thing. The main thing is that there are adults watching too. Lots of them. And not one of them says a word to the kid.

The whole way back to his mother's house, Jojo keeps looking over his shoulder. He disappears inside.

The day after that, the bus stops at the end of the street. Shana gets out with her baby—Jojo's baby—in the stroller. She has two big bags with her. She stashes one on the rack underneath where the boy sits. She slings the other one over her shoulder. It bulges and looks heavy. She pushes the stroller up the street on the same side as her parents' house. Of course everyone thinks that's where she's going. She's going to see her parents.

But before she gets to Ardell's house, she crosses the street and pushes the stroller up the walk to Jojo's mother's house. She leaves the stroller at the bottom of the porch steps and takes the two big bags up to the door. She presses the doorbell, and the door opens. She hands the two bags inside and then goes back down the steps. This time she picks up the stroller and carries it up onto the porch and into the house. The door closes behind her.

Up and down the street, people are staring at Jojo's mother's front door. Ardell is staring the hardest. He comes down off his porch and marches himself to Shana's parents' house. The next thing you know, Shana's father comes out of his house, crosses the street to Jojo's mother's house and presses the doorbell half a dozen times. When no one answers, he hammers on the door. Ardell is standing at the bottom of the porch steps, watching him.

"My brother is in the hospital because of him," Ardell says. "And because of her."

"You think *I* like this?" Shana's father says. "You think I like that my grandson has *him* for a father? I would rather she'd never had that baby. I—"

Shana is standing in the open door. Jojo is behind her. I can see that he's holding Benjamin in his arms.

"What are you doing here, Papa?" Shana says.

Shana's father grabs her by the arm and drags her out onto the porch.

"What are *you* doing here?" he says.

Shana looks at her father. Shana is so pretty. People around here say she should enter one of those top model contests. They say she would win for sure. I know that Shana's father thinks so too. He has always been proud of her. He always called her "my little girl," right up until she got pregnant with Jojo's baby. But he loves her—you can tell by the way he looks at her. And now he says all the time that the child looks just like its mother, and you can tell that makes him happy. My mother says she's sure it would be different if every time Shana's father looked at his grandson, he found himself looking at Jojo. She says the thing that saves that child from being an outcast in his own family is that he doesn't look anything like his daddy.

Shana's father says, "Get the baby and come out of there right now before everyone starts to think—"

"Before they start to think what?" Shana says.

"Just come out of there," Shana's father says.

"Benjamin is visiting his other family," Shana says. "We'll come out when we're finished." She steps back into the house where Jojo is still holding the boy. Benjamin reaches out and pulls Jojo's nose. Jojo makes a funny face. Shana laughs. The door closes behind her.

Shana's father stands there a moment, staring at the closed door like he can't believe what has just happened. He comes down the porch steps.

"You should tell your daughter to stay away from him," Ardell says.

"You should have a daughter and watch her grow into a woman and then try to tell her anything," Shana's father says.

"My brother's in the hospital because of her," Ardell says.

"Your brother's in the hospital because of Jojo," Shana's father says. "And don't you forget it."

He walks back across the street and stands in front of his house, waiting for Shana to appear. He waits for more than an hour. When Shana finally comes across the street, he takes the child from her. The whole way up his front walk, he talks to Shana. I can't hear what he says, but I can tell he's mad. He looks at Jojo's mother's house before he goes inside.

That evening, Jojo's mother is outside under the umbrella. She looks older now, but she smiles when Jojo brings her a tray of food. I hear her say, "That child looks more like you every day."

Jojo smiles.

Chapter Eight

I hear shouting and look out the front window. It's coming from across the street, from Ardell's house. A lot of people are outside. Their heads all turn in the direction of the shouting, but whatever is going on is going on inside the house. Because I have nothing else to do, I go outside too.

The front door of Ardell's house opens and Ardell's father is propelled out, backwards. He stumbles and almost falls down the porch steps. Ardell comes out of the house.

His face is twisted with anger. He pushes his father. His father grabs the railing that runs up along the steps so that Ardell can't knock him down.

"No way," Ardell yells at him. "No way."

Ardell's mother comes out of the house behind Ardell. She is wiping her eyes with a wad of tissue. She grabs one of Ardell's arms and says something to him. Ardell shakes her off. She grabs hold of him again, and again she says something to him. Ardell shoves his father, but his father hangs on tight. Ardell kicks one of the plastic chairs his mother has set out in a row on the porch. It flies up over the railing and lands in one of the rose bushes his mother is so proud of. Then he storms down the steps, shoving his father again, hard. Heads turn to watch him stomp down the street and out of sight.

Ardell's mother goes to Ardell's father and says something to him. Then she starts to cry. He puts his arms around her. It's the first time I've seen him do that since he moved out. They go back into the house together, also a first.

I walk down to the sidewalk, where Megan Dalia's mother is standing with a watering can, watering the pots of flowers that sit alongside her front walk.

"Is everything okay?" I say, nodding across the street to Ardell's house.

"The hospital says that Eden is brain-dead," she says. "There's no hope. They want to turn off the machines."

"Are they going to do it?"

"I don't think they have any choice."

I look up at Jojo's mother's house. The front window is open. A curtain flutters in the breeze. I wonder if Jojo knows what's going on. If he does, I wonder what he thinks. Does he care what he did to Eden? Does he feel bad? Does he think he's paid for what he did? Two years—it never seemed like much for putting Eden in a coma all this time. It seems like even less now.

Chapter Nine

For the next couple of days, no one sees Ardell. No one sees Jojo either, but that's because Jojo is going out the back way now.

There is a fence around his mother's small backyard, just like there are fences around all the small backyards on the street. Behind the fence is an alley. The same alley runs behind all the houses on my side of the street. If you walk along in either direction, it takes you to the street. But before you get to the

street at either end, you reach the alleys that run behind the houses on those streets.

I see Jojo leave the house by the back door, walk through his mother's yard, go out the little gate at the back and disappear into the alley. He's always gone for a long time, and when he comes back, his mother's big cloth bag is bulging. I figure he is taking the bus out of the neighborhood to do his shopping now. I wonder if anyone else knows.

Then one day, Ardell's father drives up to Ardell's house in his car. He gets out, goes up onto the porch and rings the doorbell. Ardell's mother comes out. She is dressed in her best, with a hat on her head. Ardell is dressed nicely too. He refuses to look at his father. He and his mother walk down to the car. Ardell helps his mother into the backseat. Then he climbs in beside her. Ardell's father gets in front. He looks like a chauffeur or a taxi driver, not a member of the family.

When they all come back a couple of hours later, Ardell's mother is crying. Ardell has to support her as she walks back to the house. Ardell's father sits in his car at the curb

for a few minutes. I see him wipe his eyes before he drives away.

That night my mother tells me, "Eden has passed. The funeral is the day after tomorrow."

Everybody on the street who ever knew Eden turns out for the funeral. Well, almost everyone. I see Shana's mother and father, but I don't see Shana.

A lot of people who don't live on our street also show up. Eden was popular. He was a good guy. People from his old school show up. So do people he played sports with. The church is packed with old people and young people and people in between. My mother approves of the turnout.

"A mother likes to know her son was well-thought-of," she says. "It says a lot about a person how many people come out to pay their respects."

After the funeral, people go back to the church basement, where the church ladies serve refreshments. People file up to Eden's mother and father to tell them how sorry they are and to say how they remember Eden.

Everybody has some little story about him that they tell. Eden's mother is crying the whole time, but she hugs every person who comes to talk to her, and she thanks them for coming. That night, Ardell's father's car stays parked at the curb in front of Ardell's house all night. It's still there in the morning. Ardell sits on the porch staring at it when he isn't staring at Jojo's house.

Chapter Ten

Things get turned upside down. For a couple of days after the funeral, Ardell's father's car is sitting at the curb in front of Ardell's house every night. The Saturday after the funeral, when Ardell's father drives up, he opens the trunk of the car and starts taking out boxes and suitcases. He's moving back into the house.

Ardell spends most of his time out on the porch staring at Jojo's house. But Jojo never comes out—not the front way, anyway.

Then, the same as every week, the bus stops at the corner and Shana gets down with her baby in the stroller. She's got a big bulky bag slung over her shoulder again and another one stashed under the stroller seat. This time she walks on Jojo's side of the street. She pushes the stroller up to Jojo's mother's front walk.

Ardell comes down off the porch when he sees her. He runs across the street, but he's wearing sneakers, so he doesn't make a sound. He comes up behind Shana and grabs her by one arm and spins her around. He says, "You weren't at my brother's funeral."

Shana looks surprised to see Ardell standing there, so close to her that she has to bend her head back a little so that she can look up into his eyes.

"You're hurting my arm," she says. Her voice is nice and calm.

Ardell lets go of her. "You weren't at my brother's funeral," he says again.

"I know," she says, still nice and calm. "The baby was sick. I called your mother and talked to her. Didn't she tell you?"

"Calling someone and talking to them on the phone isn't the same as coming to a funeral," Ardell says. "You, of all people, should have been at that church. You should have been at the cemetery to see him get lowered into the ground."

"I'm sorry I couldn't make it," Shana says. She sounds sincere. "But when I woke up that morning, Benjamin had a fever. I had to take him to the doctor. I'm sorry how things turned out for Eden. I told your mother that. I'm sorry how everything turned out. And if Benjamin hadn't got sick that morning, I would have been there. You know I would have, Ardell."

Ardell looks down at the child, who is squirming in his stroller, demanding to get out. He probably wants to run around, the way kids do.

"Jojo was right about one thing," Ardell says. "You should have got rid of that baby while you had the chance."

Shana stares at him, like she can't believe the words that have just come out of his mouth.

"He's my son," she says, fierce as a mother lion now. "Don't talk like that in front of him. And don't talk like that to me. He's *my* son. He's got nothing to do with you."

"He's Jojo's son," Ardell says. "And he's the reason my brother is dead. If Eden hadn't come out of the house that morning to help you, if he'd let Jojo do what he was going to do, maybe you wouldn't have that baby. For sure my brother would still be alive."

Shana is almost shaking now, she's that mad.

"I'm grateful for what Eden did," she says. "I'm grateful every single day when I wake up and see my baby. And I'm sorry for what happened—"

Smack! Ardell slaps her across the face. He slaps her so hard that her head snaps back and she stumbles. The only thing that stops her from falling is the stroller. She grabs onto the handles to steady herself.

The sound of that smack resounds up and down the street. People who had been watching Ardell step a little closer now.

People who hadn't been watching turn and look to see what happened.

Shana is clinging to the handles of the stroller. Ardell comes toward her, his fists clenched now. The child looks up at him and smiles and gurgles. For some reason, this makes Ardell even madder. He ducks down and, just like that, unsnaps the harness that's holding the child in the stroller. He picks Benjamin up and holds him at arm's length. Shana yells at him to put the baby down. She reaches for him, but Ardell swings around, holding the boy higher, out of her reach.

Benjamin whoops. He sounds happy. But Shana screams at Ardell. "Give me back my baby! Give me back my baby!"

A couple of the people who have been watching move toward Ardell. Mr. Jenson, who lives two doors down from Ardell and who is a night security guard at a mall, tells Ardell to give the child back to its mother. Ardell just stares at him. He looks at the child, and all I see is hate in his eyes.

I come down my front walk. I don't know why. Ardell is way bigger than me, and besides, my foot is in a cast. But I come down anyway. On my way to the sidewalk, I glance at Jojo's mother's house. The windows are open, and the curtains flutter in the breeze.

"Give her back the baby," people are saying.

Ardell's father appears, as if from nowhere.

"Give her back the baby, son," he says.

Ardell turns to look at him. "Son?" he says. "Did you just call me son? How can I be your son when I don't have a father? I haven't had a father since you decided you wanted my brother dead."

"Please, Ardell," his father says. "Give the girl her baby."

Ardell shakes Benjamin, just a little, as if he's been wondering what the child will do. Benjamin smiles at him. Ardell shakes him again, a little harder.

Shana screams at him, "Give me back my baby."

Maybe it's the shaking or maybe it's the screaming—the baby stops smiling and starts crying. He reaches out his little hands for his mother. Everyone is telling Ardell to give the baby back.

Then the cops show up—two of them in a patrol car. They both get out. People back away from Ardell. One of the cops goes straight to Ardell. The other one hangs back, watching. The cop who's up close to Ardell tells Ardell to give him the baby.

Ardell turns around slowly to look at the cop.

"Give me the baby," the cop says again.

Ardell hands over the baby.

Shana is practically hysterical as she takes Benjamin from the cop. One side of her face is swollen up.

The cop asks Ardell to step over to the police car. Ardell doesn't want to go. The cop's face hardens. He orders Ardell over to the police car. He puts Ardell in the backseat, where he can't get out. Then the two cops talk to Shana and to a lot of other people about what happened. When they leave, they still have Ardell in the back of the police car.

As I watch them go, I wonder how they knew to come in the first place. I wonder who called them. I look at the window that's open in Jojo's mother's house and at the curtain that's fluttering in the breeze.

Chapter Eleven

Ardell hit Shana. Ardell took Shana's baby and shook him and wouldn't give him back. Ardell didn't listen the first time the cop told him to hand over the baby and the first time he was told to step over to the police car. But everybody blames Jojo.

They say things like:

"A boy is dead. They should have locked Jojo up for longer."

"If he hadn't come back here, none of this would have happened."

"Ardell is a good boy. He did what he did because Jojo drove him to it."

"People like Jojo have no business in this neighborhood."

The police charge Ardell with assaulting both Shana and the baby. Then they let him go with a promise to appear. Most of the time, Ardell sits on his porch again and stares across the street at Jojo's house. But he also walks down to where the stores and restaurants are and talks to the storeowners and the restaurant owners.

I am in the video store when Ardell comes in. It's one of those chain places. I am checking out the new releases. Ardell asks to talk to the manager. He asks the manager if he heard what happened to his brother, who was beaten up two years ago and who just recently died of his injuries.

"Yeah, I heard something about that," the manager says.

Ardell pulls out a piece of paper and unfolds it. From where I am standing, I can see it's got a picture of a face on it. I can't actually see the face, but I know it's Jojo.

Ardell says, "This is the guy who killed my brother. They locked him up for two years, and now he is back. A bunch of us who live around here and a lot of the people who have businesses on this street have got together. We don't want this piece of garbage living in our neighborhood."

"I don't see how you can stop a person from living where he wants to live," the manager says.

"I'll tell you how," Ardell says. He describes how Mr. Brisebois at the grocery store locks his door whenever he sees Jojo coming. He says that the man who runs the take-out chicken place has told his people not to serve Jojo. He says that the pizza place won't deliver to Jojo's house. Neither will the Mexican place.

"I just run this store," the manager says. "I don't own it. I have a policy manual this thick." He holds his thumb and forefinger a few inches apart. "I have to do what the manual says, and the manual says that we're here to serve our customers."

"The people in this neighborhood have been your customers for a long time," Ardell says. "And they're serious about this guy. If you want to keep all your customers—all your *loyal* customers—you have to make them happy."

He hands the manager the piece of paper with Jojo's picture on it. "This is the guy," he says. "And I can promise you that if your loyal customers see him with one of your DVDs, they are going to find some place else to rent their movies."

After Ardell leaves, the manager takes a long look at Jojo's face on the paper. He takes it over to the cash and shows it to the cashier. He tells the cashier, "If this guy comes in here, you call me. Let me handle it."

I wonder what he will do.

Chapter Twelve

It doesn't matter what Ardell does, because Jojo hardly ever comes out onto the street. He keeps slipping out through the alley to get whatever he needs. Ardell sits outside and sits outside, but he never sees Jojo.

Well, almost never. Jojo answers the door whenever Shana comes to visit. He scoops the baby out of her arms and swings it up high. Benjamin laughs. Once I hear Jojo call him "my little man." Shana smiles.

Jojo also comes out at the exact same time every Wednesday morning. On those days, he has his mother with him, and they walk together to the curb to get into a taxi that Jojo must have ordered. They leave. They always return a few hours later. When Jojo's mother gets out of the taxi again, she always leans heavily on Jojo. She looks really sick. On those days, she never comes out to sit under her umbrella.

"Poor woman," my mother says one day.

"What's wrong with her?" I ask.

My mother looks at me.

"She's sick, isn't she?" I say.

My mother doesn't answer.

"What does she have?" I ask.

My mother studies me. Finally she says, "She doesn't want people to know about it."

"Know about what?"

"You know how people talk around here," my mother says.

"I won't tell," I say. "Is she dying?"

My mother looks stunned by the question, but she nods. "Probably," she says. "She has cancer. She's taking treatment, but I don't think there's anything they can do. It's spread too much. She's lucky that Jojo is back."

That's the first time I ever heard anyone say that someone is lucky Jojo is back.

"He's looking after her," my mother says. "He cooks for her and does all the cleaning. He takes her to her appointments and holds her hand the whole time."

Now it's my turn to be surprised.

"I see her at the hospital most times when she comes in," she says. "I see him with her. Sometimes I talk to her. You know, if most people saw him do what the people at the hospital see him do, they would have a different opinion. I'm not saying what he did was right, because it wasn't. I'm not even saying that he's changed since he went away, because I don't know if that's true or not. But he's a good son. He looks after his mother. I don't think there's anything he wouldn't do for her. And lately he talks to her about the baby and about Shana. I know he's sorry he ever told Shana she shouldn't have that baby."

She looks hard at me. "He was a wild boy, there's no doubt about that. He caused a lot of people a lot of problems and a lot of heartache, including his mother. But he's making up for it now, without anyone watching him, without anyone knowing."

Chapter Thirteen

Wednesday rolls around again. It's a hot day, so I am sitting outside, trying to catch some breeze. My leg inside the cast is itching like crazy. I wonder what I can shove down there to scratch it. Across the street, Ardell is sitting on his porch. But this morning he isn't alone. There are a bunch of his friends on the porch with him. They are all staring at the street.

I can see by my watch that it's time for Jojo and his mother to go to the hospital. Sure enough, I see a taxi turn onto the street.

It's coming toward Jojo's house nice and slow, because there are always kids playing on the street this time of year. But before the taxi gets to Jojo's house, Ardell comes down off his porch and waves it down. He makes a motion to get the driver to roll down his window, and then he bends down so that he can talk to the driver.

I see the driver shake his head.

Ardell's friends stand in front of the taxi, blocking it.

Ardell says something else to the taxi driver. Again I see the driver shake his head. A couple of Ardell's friends press in even closer to the taxi. Ardell pulls out a piece of paper, the one with Jojo's picture on it. I bet he is telling the taxi driver the same thing he told the manager of the video store. But the driver is arguing back. Driving a taxi is a hard way to make a living. The driver wants his fare.

I don't know what Ardell says that finally does the trick, but the next thing you know, the driver backs up the taxi and starts to turn it around. That's when the door to Jojo's mother's house opens, and Jojo comes out.

He runs down the porch steps, yelling at the taxi to "Come back! Hey, come back!" But it doesn't. It drives away.

Jojo is on the sidewalk now. Ardell and his friends are standing in the middle of the street. They stare at each other. Jojo hesitates. Then he goes out into the street where Ardell is. Jojo's hands are balled up into fists. I can see the muscles in his neck. But he is trying to stay calm.

"I told you I don't want trouble," Jojo says. "But if you want to press on me, you can go right ahead. My ma, though, that's different. That taxi was for her. She needs to get to an appointment."

"Yeah?" Ardell says. "Well, my brother was trying to get himself to college, and look what happened."

Jojo looks right into Ardell's eyes. He says, "My ma is old, and she's sick. You got something against me, I guess that's your business. But my ma never did anything to hurt you or anyone in your family."

Ardell looks right back at Jojo. "Nothing," he says, "but bring you into this world."

Right then, Ardell's mother comes outside. She stands on the porch for a minute, looking at what is happening in the street. I see a worried look on her face. She comes down the front walk toward Ardell and his friends. Ardell hasn't noticed her. Neither has Jojo.

"I'm going back inside, and I'm going to call another taxi for my ma," Jojo says.

"You do that," Ardell says, "and see where it gets you."

Ardell's mother has come around behind Jojo, probably so that she can see Ardell's face. She touches Jojo's arm, I think to get him to move out of the way. But Jojo hasn't seen her. He doesn't know who is touching his arm. All he knows is that he is standing in the middle of the street surrounded by Ardell's friends and that his mother's taxi is gone and Ardell is going to do what he can to make another one go away. And now someone is touching his arm. But the way Jojo reacts, you'd think someone grabbed his arm and was getting ready to twist it hard.

Jojo swings around and, *bam*, his hands fly out and hit Ardell's mother in the chest.

She wasn't expecting this. A woman like her would never expect to get hit by someone like Jojo. She falls right over and lands on her back in the street.

That does it. Ardell gets right into it. He's got the excuse he's been looking for. He sees his mother lying there in the street. She's dazed. She's hurt too. You can tell because she's having trouble getting herself to a seated position, never mind standing up again.

But Ardell doesn't go to help her. No, his eyes are blazing at Jojo. He rushes forward, his fists up. He's going to pound on Jojo, and his friends are going to help him. But then someone grabs Ardell.

It's his father.

Ardell's father grabs Ardell and spins him around. He says, "We just buried your brother, and you're out here looking for more trouble?"

Ardell tries to shake him off, but his father holds tight. He drags Ardell to the sidewalk on the far side of the street. He yells at Ardell's friends to use their heads. He tells some of them to keep Ardell off the street.

He tells some other ones to help Ardell's mother up. He yells at Jojo, "Get out of here. Just get out of here. You've been nothing but trouble ever since you learned to walk. Get out of here and let decent people go about their business."

Jojo stares at him. Jojo, who used to be so tough that people would cross the street when they saw him coming, has a hurt look on his face. He opens his mouth like he wants to explain his side of the story. But in the end, all he does is shake his head. He goes over to where Ardell's mother is. She is on her feet now, and one of Ardell's friends is holding her by the elbow.

"I'm sorry, Mrs. Withrow," Jojo says. "I didn't see it was you." And it was true—he didn't. "I'm sorry."

Ardell's mother looks up at him. Then she does what I've never seen a grown woman do before—she spits at him. And right then, for the first time, I feel sorry for Jojo.

Chapter Fourteen

Half an hour later, a car pulls up outside Jojo's house. Ardell, who is up on his porch again, sees it and stands up. His father comes out of the house and gives him a look.

Ardell stays on the porch and peers at the car. I don't think he recognizes the driver. I sure don't. All I can tell is that it's a woman. I don't think Ardell can see the front-seat passenger from where he is either. But I can. It's Shana. The driver honks the horn, and Jojo and his mother come out and

get into the backseat of the car. The car
drives away.

A couple of hours later, a taxi pulls
up—it's a different company this time—and
Jojo helps his mother out. She leans heavily
on him. He takes her up the walk and into the
house. Ardell watches them.

All afternoon there is a buzz on the street.
People stroll over to their neighbors' houses
or wander across the street to talk to other
neighbors who are outside. They all nod at
Ardell's house, so it's pretty obvious that they
are all talking about what happened. A few
women who know Ardell's mother well go
to the house and disappear inside. When they
come out, other women drift toward them
to find out how Ardell's mother is and what
exactly happened.

Word gets around.

That night when the sun is going down,
Jojo comes out the front door. He doesn't
go out the back way. He holds himself up
tall, like he's trying to make a point. He
walks down the street, right past Ardell's
house. Ardell and all his friends are up on

the porch again. They have been there since late afternoon. They've ordered pizzas and eaten them and have been horsing around out there ever since. They get quiet when they see Jojo go by.

Ardell stands up. The friends of his who have been sitting get to their feet. They all come down off the porch and follow Jojo down the street. But this time there's something different on Ardell's face and something different about the way he's walking. He stares straight at the back of Jojo's head. He walks right in step with Jojo. He makes fists with his hands. The rest of them walk the same way.

This time, none of the neighbors follow. It doesn't turn into a parade the way it did that first time. This time, when people see Ardell and his friends walk down the street grim-faced behind Jojo, they retreat to their porches.

Not me.

I have a feeling that something is going to happen. I make my way down the sidewalk on the other side of the street. When Jojo and

Ardell and the rest of them turn the corner, I turn the corner. Jojo keeps walking until he gets to the drugstore near the park.

Jojo goes into the drugstore. Ardell and his friends wait outside. When Jojo comes out, he's carrying a little white paper bag, the kind they put prescriptions in. I bet it's something for his mother. He starts to go back the way he came. But Ardell and his friends block his way. So Jojo wheels around like it's no big deal and walks toward the park.

The park is a big one. To get into it, you have to walk down some stairs from the sidewalk because the park is way down low compared to most of the streets around it. Most people call it the pit instead of the park. It has a baseball diamond and a soccer field. It has a swimming pool and a wading pool. In winter it has a skating rink. It also has a playground with swings and slides for little kids, and benches where their parents can sit and watch them. Along one side there are trees and bushes where it's nice and shady and where people go if they want to do something and not be seen. Guys take girls in there. People say that drugs are sold in there. They say, "Who knows what else goes on in there."

Jojo starts to walk past the park, but when he gets to the stairs, Ardell catches him and shoves him. Jojo stumbles and disappears from sight. Ardell starts down the stairs. His friends follow him. By the time I get there, all of them are down near the bottom.

There aren't many lights down there. The city and the cops don't want people going down there at night. Who knows what they might do. And it's too hard for the cops to get down there. Because it's so dark, there aren't many people down there. The few I can see are little dark smudges. I can't make out their faces. I can't make out much about them. If I hadn't seen Jojo and Ardell and the rest of them go down there, I wouldn't know it was them. It's too hard to see.

I stand at the top of the stairs and watch them move across the park toward the trees and the bushes where no one will be able to see them. I can't be sure, but it looks like they are pushing Jojo over there. A couple of times I see someone fall. I'm pretty sure it's Jojo. Then I see someone bend down and drag him up again. At least, that's the way I imagine it. Maybe I'm wrong. Maybe Jojo is being helped up, not dragged up. Maybe it isn't even Jojo who fell.

Then they all disappear behind the trees and bushes. I stand at the top of the stairs, waiting. I stand there for what seems like a long time. No one comes back. I tell myself that there are a lot of ways out of the park. They could all be home by now.

Finally I turn and make my way home too.

Chapter Fifteen

The next morning while I am at the hospital getting my cast looked at, the cops show up at Jojo's mother's house. They tell her that Jojo is dead. They say that he was hit on the head with a rock. I find this out from Megan Dalia's mother when I come back from the fracture clinic at the hospital. My mother is still at work.

"The police went up and down the street, asking people if they know who would have killed Jojo," Megan's mother tells me.

When I ask her what people said, she says, "Near as I can tell, they all said the same thing. They said Jojo was no good. They said no one around here liked him and it's too bad they let him out so soon after what he did. But they said they don't know who killed him. They didn't see anything. No one saw anything."

I want to ask her "What about you?" But something stops me.

That night, while I'm watering my mother's flowers for her while she does a double shift, Ardell's father walks across the street. He stands on the sidewalk watching me for a few minutes. Then he says, "Those are pretty flowers."

"That's my mother's doing," I say. "Not mine. I don't know the first thing about flowers."

He smiles at me and nods. A few moments later, he says, "I saw you walk down the street last night after Jojo."

I look at him.

"I'm glad Ardell was home all night last night with me and his mother," he says. "I'm glad all his friends were home safe too. So is everyone around here. Otherwise, the police might think that Ardell had something to do with what happened to Jojo, and that would be a shame, wouldn't it?

"Ardell's going to college this year. It's a miracle he got the grades he did, he was so broken up about what happened to Eden. It would be a shame if the police thought he had anything to do with Jojo. It would be a shame to see a good boy's life ruined over someone like that."

He stands there a little longer, watching me. Then he goes back across the street.

I wait to see what happens.

Nothing does.

Ardell comes and goes at his mother's house, like usual. People nod at him and wave at him—the same people who turned and went back onto their porches when Ardell and the rest of them followed Jojo down the street to the drugstore.

I think about that walk. I wonder if anyone up near the drugstore saw Ardell following Jojo. I wonder if any of them will say anything to the police. Then I remember all those pictures of Jojo that Ardell showed around. I remember him talking to all those shopkeepers. If even one of them talks to the cops, maybe the cops will take another look at Ardell.

Still nothing happens.

One day a taxi arrives in front of Jojo's mother's house and Shana gets out. She is dressed in black. She goes up to the house and gets Jojo's mother. She's dressed in black too. They get into the taxi.

I think, *They're going to Jojo's funeral, and they're going alone.*

Later, Megan Dalia's mother tells me the police have been around again. She says they keep asking about Ardell, but everyone tells them the same thing—they don't know anything. Besides, Megan's mother says, Ardell's parents say that Ardell was home all night that night.

I think about that. I think about what Ardell's father said to me. I think about all

the people on our street. I think about Eden
Withrow and how he's dead because of
Jojo. I think of Jojo and how he's dead now.
I think about how everyone thinks that Ardell
is a good person, even now. I think about
the two years Jojo did for the life he ruined.
Then I think about Ardell again, about what
he did and what he knows and what he thinks
he knows.

Chapter Sixteen

Two weeks after Jojo's funeral, Shana knocks on our door. My mother isn't home, so I answer.

Shana is standing on our porch with the baby in her arms. She tells me that she's going up and down the street talking to everyone. She says she lived on this street long enough to know that everyone sees everything and not the other way around. She tells me how sorry she is about Eden, but that Jojo had changed and that he even drew comfort from his son. She tells me how heartbroken his mother is, as heartbroken as Eden's mother. She tells me taking a life for any reason is wrong. She says she is telling me what she has told everyone else—if I know anything, I should tell. She says she hopes I will think about what she has said.

I think all night.

I think about this neighborhood and what it can do to people.

I think about *my* mother. I am all she has.

I think about her house. She has lived here since before I was born. This is *her* neighborhood. Everyone knows her. I think about what could happen, how people might treat her.

The next morning, I call the police and tell them what I know. And then I brace myself because I know that everything is about to change for me.

Norah McClintock is the author of a number of novels, including *Tell*, *Down*, *Bang*, *Snitch*, *Watch Me* and *Marked*. Norah lives in Toronto, Ontario.

Orca Soundings

Orca Soundings

Orca Soundings

Orca Soundings

Bang

978-1-55143-654-8 • $9.95 • PB
978-1-55143-656-2 • $16.95 CDN • $14.95 US • LIB

Orca Soundings

Down

978-1-55143-766-8 • $9.95 • PB
978-1-55143-768-2 • $16.95 CDN • $14.95 US • LIB

Orca Soundings

Snitch

978-1-55143-484-1 • $9.95 • PB

Orca Soundings

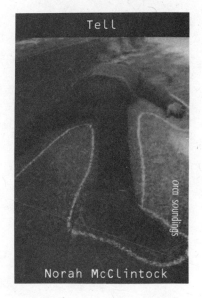

Tell

Tell

978-1-55143-511-4 • $9.95 • PB

Orca Currents

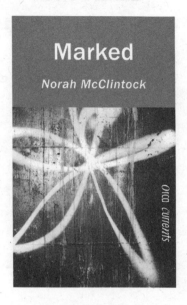

Marked

978-1-55143-992-1 • $9.95 • PB
978-1-55143-994-5 • $16.95 • LIB

Orca Currents

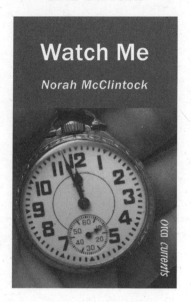

Watch Me

978-1-55469-039-8 • $9.95 • PB
978-1-55469-040-4 • $16.95 • LIB